WHOLEHEARTED HALF-TRUTHS

Collected Prose Poems

Melanie Reed

Wholehearted Half-Truths
by Melanie Reed

All rights reserved. No part of this publication may be reproduced or transmitted in any form or by any means, electronic or mechanical, including photocopying or recording or by any information storage and retrieval systems, without expressed written consent of the author and/or artists.

All characters herein are fictitious, and any resemblance between them and actual people is strictly coincidental.

Poem copyrights owned by Melanie Reed
Cover art "Head in Clouds" by Melanie Reed
Cover design by Laura Givens

First Printing, November 2023

Hiraeth Publishing
P.O. Box 1248
Tularosa, NM 88352

e-mail: hiraethsubs@yahoo.com

Visit www.hiraethsffh.com for science fiction, fantasy, horror, scifaiku, and more. While you are there, visit the Shop for books and more! **Support the small, independent press...**

TABLE OF CONTENTS

5	Towns
19	Travel
22	House and Home
30	Family
34	Jobs
38	Health
43	Relationships
53	Therapy
64	Life
70	Bitterness
75	Art
91	Words
105	Announcements
113	Jokes
121	Debatable
125	The World
132	God
137	Uneasy
142	Fate
147	Endings

TOWNS

Urban Renewal

In this town, they renamed all the streets in the course of a year. Having realized that most of the old names related either to people that no one remembered, currently inapplicable forms of city self-promotion, or to various repetitive forms of words like "lake," "field," "crest," "hill," "brook," "side," "cliff," "forest," "view," or "park," a series of committees tried to come up with better names. The first committee mostly consisted of pet shelter volunteers who prided themselves on the art of efficient speed-naming. But to simply have myriad street names with monikers like "Cuddles," "Aloysius," or "Tiger" was simply to exchange one problem for another. The second committee came mostly from nurses at a foundling hospital. Many of these volunteers had big chunks of the latest editions of baby name books memorized, and were anxious to put this quirky talent to use. But problems arose when some of the residential families wanted to name their streets after *their* kids. At last a committee emerged of people with English degrees. Having an intrinsic appreciation for the timeless and unique qualities of titles like "The Metamorphosis," "The Iceman Cometh," and "The Wasteland," this group did a bang-up job. If you're ever in town, you should visit the riverside walk, now named "Violet Attar of Bitter Rose."

Permission to Come Aboard

After being banned from almost every social setting for their outrageous behavior, a group of fools decided to band together to charter a ship that circumnavigated their island town. In this ongoing one-vessel parade, they were free to be who they were. After a while, the townspeople started missing the fools, and reacted by banning the wise people for their over-seriousness. These new exiles were smart enough to know a good thing when they saw it, and chartered their own ship. At this point, the remaining townspeople began to start missing the two extremes that had made their town so unique, and sent off some flares of forgiveness. But both the fools and the wise men had been burned too many times to fall for that. Finally, the townspeople had no other option but to charter their own boat, in the hope of at least getting to visit the ships of the wise men and fools.

Good Fences

Heartily sick of the chaos in their town from idealistic unity followed by reactive repudiation, a group of town planners took matters into their own hands. From then on, at age 18, everyone in the town received one chair, half a table, half a couch, half a bed, a collapsible plasterboard wall extension, and a small storage unit – all identically sized and shaped, but each stamped with a personal one-of-a-kind design. Couples who moved in together could combine their items to share, but would never lose out should they decide to break up. Even if no single-person dwellings were available immediately, they could simply put up their wall extensions to create a private space. For people who wanted to travel or who were still living with their parents, their furniture could always be stored for free. These policies proved to be so popular, that other towns quickly adopted them. Eventually the practice spread to cities, states, and in some cases, even countries, though it was kind of tricky dividing up the land masses.

Suspended Sentences

In this town, word pollution was at an all-time high. With so many people flooding in every day, the townspeople were choking in the word-clogged atmosphere, and spent so much time crawling through the ever-growing word jungles that productivity was at an all-time low. Words also crashed into each other constantly, leaving piles of ruined sentences bleeding on the sides of the roads. It seemed somewhat drastic, but the plan went through to limit public word flow by 50 percent over the course of a year. Many public word paths were removed or consolidated, and special express-word paths were installed for people to double up and share words, with one person speaking for four, instead of everyone talking wastefully at the same time.

Eliminations

The edict came down that teakettles were now off limits. The people grumbled a bit, but quickly found creative workarounds, such as heating their water in saucepans or in their microwaves. A few months later, it was decreed that chairs were now off limits. This was even less convenient, but the people eventually became flexible enough to sit, lean or stand in different places and different ways. Only two weeks later, it was proclaimed that hands were now off limits. This was much harder to adapt to, but the people had no choice but to eliminate any activities that required the use of their hands. Three days later, the people received the announcement that brains were now off limits. It was the last announcement they ever heard.

Ghost Town

In this town, the number of ghosts was well above the average. In fact, there were more ghosts than people. This posed a problem, because since ghosts feel most comfortable when they're actually haunting a person, ghost fights over "hauntees" broke out frequently. Finally a system was devised whereby each ghost had to take a number and wait in line till the next hauntee was free, and each haunting could only last three or four minutes. But with so much haunting, the hauntees began leaving town. Finally the ghosts were forced to just haunt each other.

Progress

In this town, things often seem different. Whole buildings spring up out of nowhere, while others disappear. Entire communities abruptly vanish, while new ones crop up in their place. Words and phrases once cherished are no longer understood.

Reluctant Resurrection

In this town, they take multiple life sentences seriously. When a prisoner dies, his body is cryogenically frozen so he can start his next life sentence when science gets sufficiently advanced.

Aging Relatively

In this town, people live longer but mature slower. Toddlers till their 20s, they attend public school through their 40s, begin some form of higher education in their 60s, and develop families and careers typically in their 80s. For women, the 80s and 90s are the prime child-bearing years. Sadly, the same kinds of skewed male/female dynamics prevail as do those in other towns. While a spry gentleman of 130 can still have a respectable relationship with a woman in her early 100s, it's looked on askance for a women of 125 to be with a younger man of only 115.

Indelible

Half the people in this town have birthmarks inside of their brains. Compulsory x-rays in childhood detect them, but as part of a study of whether ignorance is bliss, nobody is told their results.

Absence Makes the Heart

In this town, intimacy runs backwards. Total strangers start right off having deep conversations, sex and cohabitation. From there, they progress cautiously toward small talk, insincere hugs, and separate vacations. Upper-middle levels of closeness rate quick handshakes, separate houses and brief nods. After a decade or two of hard intimacy work, the apex of closeness is reached: separate neighborhoods and a Christmas card once a year.

Unhappy Returns

In this town, they take birthdays seriously. Every home and office has a special birthday room. The room is programmed to flash the birthday person's name in blinking lights, followed by a recorded message directing them to enter. In lieu of decorations, cake, ice cream or presents, this room contains a logbook in which the birthday person is tasked with recording their failures, successes, sins and losses of the previous year, and their resolutions, expectations, hopes and fears for the year ahead. In lieu of the "Happy Birthday" song, each birthday person is then required to read the entry aloud to their family members, neighbors, or coworkers and be willing to consider any additions, deletions or corrections that are advised.

Multi-Story Building

This town's library was designed around virtual story immersions, since that's what its residents preferred. Like conventional libraries, it was divided into age-themed sections. In the "younger readers" section, a bustling hubbub of piles of check-ins and check-outs, most of the experiences were based around adventures. The adults section, with a less heavily-trafficked but steadier flow, was comprised of mysteries. What would the "mature readers" section consist of? I wondered, and being older myself, I hastened to peruse it. Here I found a much smaller section, where many of the experiences had apparently been checked out but never returned – perhaps because their readers had either died or been dissatisfied with the selections. I picked up a couple of the remaining selections. They were all joke books. Had anyone died laughing?

TRAVEL

Downsized Excursions

First she traveled the world. Next she explored her own state. Finally it occurred to her to check out the city she lived in, ending with an in-depth examination of her own neighborhood and its many distinguishing features. Since her own house seemed like one of them, she created a self-guided tour of all its rooms, with sequential numbers, a painted path, signage, and dioramas. Lastly, she decided to focus on just one square foot of her living room floor. It was truly amazing how much detail was in there.

Perpetual Motion

They flew south for the winter, leaving in plenty of time before it got cold. About halfway down, they ran into a party coming their way. "What gives?" the group leader said. "It's freezing down there," said one of the party members. "We thought it would be warmer where you are." Wanting to see for himself, the leader pushed his group on, but they had to stop ten miles out because of an ice storm. After an emergency rest stop, they headed back, only to run into the same party again about ten miles out. "Your place is on fire," the other group leader said.

HOUSE AND HOME

One for All

The building management was cracking down. First, only one pet at a time per tenant, then only one roommate per every resident's tenancy, and finally only one pet per every resident's tenancy. Long-term residents whose pets died and roommates left got lonelier and lonelier. Finally, a new unwritten policy developed whereby every new tenant with a roommate or a pet was required to share them out for their first year. Should the roommates or pets be cranky or infirm, the new tenants themselves would have to share themselves out.

Too Familiar

The "free pile" lived in the basement of her building – a designated area where tenants could drop off, trade or acquire unwanted items. One day she came across a delightful whatnot, only to realize that it once was hers. How could they have disposed of such a special thing? she thought. Stricken by donator's regret, she picked it up again.

Happy Events

Since the new baby kept them up all night anyway, an enterprising couple sought to offset the higher cost of their new apartment by renting out the living room as an 80s-themed event space. High-output speakers masked the cries, discarded pacifiers served the theme, and dim lights gave the crayoned wall scrawls Basquiat-like hip and edginess. For post-party cleanup, the baby was wrapped in a dishtowel and turned loose to crawl on the floor.

Inheritance

A middle-aged man inherited his father's house. A sentimental fellow, he promptly moved in himself, instead of selling. The house's value increased so much that he could afford to enlarge. When he himself died, he passed it on to his son, who did the same thing, and on and on throughout several more generations. Another even more sentimental middle-aged man inherited his own father's far inferior house, and promptly moved in as well. Since he was unable to pay for the major repairs required, the house's value decreased incrementally. When he himself died, he passed it on to his son, who did the same thing, and on and on throughout several more generations. One day, a man from the fifth or sixth generation of each these two families met each other on vacation. They both lamented the sadness of being in exile from family homes. The first man's house had grown so large that it took up most of the town, and so the commute to get out the door had finally become too long. The second man's house was down to a tiny handful of dust lying on a cracking foundation, and though the man still slept there in the summer, it was simply too cold to do so all year round.

Soiled Again

The beautification committee sent out a memo encouraging each of the building's residents to put out plant stands in the hallways outside their front doors. The residents liked the idea, but the cleaning crew complained about having to move these stands every time the hallways were cleaned. In response, the management committee put out a memo requiring residents to clean underneath their plant stands at least once every six months. When the first inspection came up, the management moved all the plant stands a foot or so to the side, exposing several residents' failure to clean. By the date of the reinspect, the guilty offenders had polished each dirty square foot to a fare-thee-well, which, intentionally or not, exposed the much lazier floor-cleaning efforts of the cleaning crew. At 3 a.m. the next morning, the cleaning crew held a meeting, and after much debate, came up with the brilliant solution of simply snipping and scattering enough plant leaves to cover the shinier spots. But at this point, everyone started to feel a little too put-upon. Management's new memo to both cleaning crew and residents to keep the leaves off the floor resulted in both groups' adamant refusal. The beautification committee threw up its hands. The price of beauty, alas, was simply too high.

The Home Complacency Test

Because most people don't want to be seen buying it, it comes in a plain white box. The symptoms creep up gradually – first with the reluctance to read the news, then with the reluctance to visit your friends, and finally the reluctance to leave your house. At this point, it may be too late to try to turn things around.

Spector of Plenty

The real estate agent assured us that the house was no longer haunted, since a full exorcism had been done right after the termite inspection. Shortly after the move-in, however, we noticed that five of our boxes had been unpacked during the night -- the contents put away in neat and logical places. Had the poltergeist been replaced by helpful elves, or was it the ghost of my mom? Nothing else happened till the end of the week, but then when we got home from work, the furniture had been moved to more appropriate places, and the next day, two paintings by famous artists appeared in the dining room. Then things started ramping up. Pretty soon there was no more room to walk freely, what with the five china cabinets, seven whatnots, twelve armchairs, and six pianos. We started an ongoing yard sale, and people flocked to the house every day and bought us out, but so many more things appeared overnight that we had to start giving them away, and finally paying to have on-call movers ready to work 24/7. We really hope these spirits start dematerializing.

FAMILY

Roots

If our family had a crest, there'd have to be a tree on it. My great-great-great-great-grandfather was a logger. My great-great-great-grandfather made hand-turned custom wood furniture. My great-great-grandfather ran a reforestation program. My great-grandfather was a soil tester, before that job became obsolete. My grandfather ran a plant that manufactured aluminum Christmas trees. My grandfather helped design all the other aluminum trees. My father was an aluminum tree installer. And I'm on the team that hangs the seasonal leaves.

Family Show

I was enjoying the show when the lead singer suddenly invited up his six-year-old daughter as a guest performer. She did a creditable job, and then disappeared backstage. Later on, his three-year-old daughter had her own brief turn in the limelight before being walked offstage by her babysitter. Finally, a pregnant woman appeared, who he introduced as his wife. He held a microphone to her stomach, and though I couldn't see or hear anything, the woman assured us that the baby was dancing.

They Grow Up So Fast

When our friends used to complain about their whiny kids, we never knew what to say. Our daughter was precociously self-sufficient. As an unweaned baby, she managed to crawl to the house of a neighbor who was also breast-feeding, to supply herself with a snack. Once she learned to read, there was no stopping her. Invited to the mall to buy a new outfit, she politely informed us that she'd bartered some of her old baby toys for a small flock of sheep, whose wool she was using to weave her own clothes. By this time, she was also growing her own fruits, herbs and vegetables, which she cooked into nutritious stews on our outdoor grill. When we asked her how she'd like us to re-decorate her room, she informed us that she'd recently installed plumbing and electricity in our shed, and was taking up pottery-throwing so she could make her own dishes. Finally, we gave up offering her things, and started pampering our two dogs instead. By the time she was 30, we'd almost forgotten about her till the day she suddenly came home and asked us to make her a BLT cut on the diagonal with lightly-toasted bread. We had to give away the dogs, because she sleeps in our bed now and there's no room for them.

JOBS

Overqualified

Abandoned by his circus in a small Midwestern town, a geek signed up for job-search counseling. The first week, his liaison gave him three promising leads. A local granary was his first stop. "Our cat just ran away," the field hand said. "Can you bite all the heads off all our rats?" "I don't do rats," the geek said. "Toxic shock." His next stop was a butcher who had chickens in the window. "Excellent!" the butcher said. "I've got a pile in back – feel free to start!" "I only do *live* chickens," said the geek. Lastly, he headed towards the edge of town. "Oh, good, I need a hand," said Dusty from the Free-Range Home Roost Coop. "My partner left and I can't do the cleaning, feeding, *and* maintain the website all at once." "I don't clean them or feed them." said the geek. "I can't bite off their heads when they're like pets." That night he had a nightmare where someone bit off *his* head. His body ran around for quite a while.

Not Just Another Average Friday

I clocked in at the entrance and kissed my sweetie goodbye. Walked in with a bit of a puffed-up chest, looking extra spiffy in my new fur coat that had just been brushed and cleaned the night before. "Hey there, Scout, who're you trying to impress?" came a jovial bark to my right. Startled, I turned, only to be confronted by a weird stranger covered with nothing but his skin. All four of his legs looked cold. "It's me, Max!" the skin-covered creature cried. "Did you forget that today is casual day?"

Productivity

I'd been starting to suspect that a lot of time and effort might be being wasted on sports, when one early season baseball game, I noticed a fan in the row in front of me working diligently on some scrimshaw. By the end of the game, he'd completed a seal, a whale and an Eskimo. At a later game, I spotted two different fans who were both making pirate ships. Last week, there was yet another new development: five men walking through the stands hawking scrimshaw supplies. I need to get in on this somehow.

HEALTH

The Medicine Game

A man came to visit an old friend whom he hadn't seen in a while and found him in bed, in pain. It seemed this mysterious ailment had been plaguing his friend for years. "Have you heard about the Jesus Pill?" the man inquired. "No, what is it?" asked his friend. "I happen to have some right here," the man announced, and pulled a bottle from his pocket. Two pills and his friend was up and walking happily around. "It's a miracle!" he cried. Unfortunately, the effects were only short-term. It also developed that they only worked when the man himself administered the medicine to his friend. This resulted in his friend following him around every day so that he could administer the pills. One day, the man's friend overheard him talking to another friend. "I've made a mint off this guy!" he heard the man say. "But he's really dogging my heels. I'm wondering if I should just admit that the pill's a placebo." Furious, his friend stormed off and immediately began working on producing his own Jesus Pill, which he then proceeded to market and sell at an excellent profit. This cheered him up so much that his own pain was forgotten.

Obligatory Test

This light shows that the things that I emit are outside normal limits – too far left, outfield, not even in the park. I pay the fee to get my innards analyzed, but fixing costs too much, so magically I get a pass to keep the whole show going one more year.

Doubling Down

She'd always wanted to get a permanent tattoo of the word "temporary," but a low pain tolerance kept her dragging her heels until the day she had to get a breast removed and bribed her doctor to let her get it done right there on the same day. "You want me to put it on the other breast?" the tattoo artist said.

Restoration Notification

Like Da Vinci's "Last Supper," the choice of poor original materials coupled with the process of time have put a unique work at risk. To prevent further degradation, and to do whatever possible to protect this work in the future, many parts of it will have to be taken completely apart, subjected to a variety of processes, and then recomposed from scratch. Although I have little in the way of specialized training, I've nevertheless been selected to be part of the restoration team, and encouraged to help in whatever ways I can. This project is funded, but only up to a point, so while I get free training, I won't be paid for my help, so am tasked with simultaneously maintaining my day job throughout. The project will no doubt be challenging, but potentially rewarding, although the work will likely never be fully restored to its original form. What makes a given work worth saving? Perhaps only time will tell. If you'd like to apply to be part of the team, please contact me at my office in the sick bay.

RELATIONSHIPS

For Better or Worse

Life and Death got married. It was an arranged marriage, further cemented by a series of inheritances dispensable only if the couple stayed together. The arguments arose mainly over the ways they spent their money. Not surprisingly, while Life preferred spacious country homes with horses and rolling hills, Death was more drawn to dark gothic castles with dungeons, towers and moats. Finally they managed to compromise on a townhome.

November-December Romance

Of course their friends wondered how it was going to turn out. May imagined that November might start wanting someone a bit spryer, and perhaps fool around with October. April surmised that December might get a little impatient with November's slightly lesser degree of experience, and force her to read two extra books a week. June wondered how their two groups of friends could ever get along, what with November hanging out mostly with fall friends and December being tighter with winter ones.

Mea Maxima Culpa

Once upon a time, there was a woman who loved to criticize and a man who hated to be criticized. Luckily, for the first couple years of their marriage, she only criticized other people. But soon after that, to no one's surprise, she started in on the man. At first he took it in stride, since she was almost always easily placated by some kind of show of agreement. But eventually her criticisms became so all-encompassing that she ran out of time to criticize during the day, and had to continue at night. Since the man couldn't employ his usual placating tactics when he was asleep, he was woken up so often that his coworkers, noticing the dark circles under his eyes, started to joke with him about having a new baby way too late in life. Finally he came up with an effective solution: a custom-designed pair of glow-in-the-dark pajamas emblazoned with the words, "Everything I ever did in life was wrong."

Dysfunctional Family Restaurant

My place has been doing great the last five years. As owner, it warms my heart to see the lines around the block – the parents screaming at their kids, the relatives unfriending other relatives, and people abusing their substance of choice right there in front of God and everyone. These poor folks need some place to go where they can be themselves. But lately the definition of dysfunction's getting too broad. When families get too quiet, I start getting a bad name. Sure, they could be raging inside, but how would anyone know? I'm thinking of handing out a door survey to weed out the out-and-out fakes.

Comfort

While his comfort zone was full of people, her comfort zone was empty. Not only that, but while his comfort zone was piled high with soft pillows in the shape of Disney characters, her comfort zone was a forest of sharp sticks. One day he came knocking at the gate of her comfort zone with a lovely stick bouquet. Through the intercom, she instructed him to slide the sticks one by one through the opening, and then find his own way out. Though she'd enjoyed the sticks, she hated the disturbance. A few days later, she set off for his comfort zone, sticks in hand. When she got there, it was so packed with people, she couldn't even see him. One by one, she poked them with her sticks to get them out of her way. Eventually she found him sprawled out on a big Snow White cushion. Although he was feeling less comfortable by the minute since his company'd started leaving, he was utterly delighted that she'd brought him the gift of herself.

Relentless Preservation

Her email memory function was a bittersweet convenience. Whereas she could obliterate the names and contact numbers of estranged friends and lovers in her physical address book with one stroke of a pen, their presence lived forever in the contact list – invisible but conjured back with one unintentional keystroke.

This Week's Observation

A pendulum swinging back and forth between indifference and hate is much easier to manage than a pendulum swinging back and forth between love and hate. Also, if you think you're swinging back and forth between indifference and love, it isn't really love.

Fun

She'd been told quite a few times that she should just have fun. But she didn't like the implication that fun is the only realistically attainable shared state, or the implication that it's dangerous to develop any attachments to those with whom fun is connected. Somehow, that all seemed more like sadness than like fun.

Love Him, Love Him Not

A group of the prospective groom's friends set up a lovely bower in the wooded glade of a park with personalized signage enjoining his prospective bride to say yes to his surprise proposal. But one of the girl's friends who was against the match had found out about the plan, and enlisted *her* friends to set up another surprise bower not far away designed for the boy to discover her refusal. However, no sooner had this second bower been set up, than a third group of friends of both the boy and girl who objected to such wholesale dismissal set up a more judicious surprise bower designed to list the conditions by which the girl *might* consider entertaining such a proposal.

THERAPY

Monster Bargain

Two women struck up a conversation in the grocery store, in the course of which it developed that one had been abducted by aliens and the other had been possessed by seven demons. After they got on the subject of medical coverage, it turned out that significantly more coverage was available for having demons than for being abducted, so after a certain amount of consideration, the woman with the demons gave the other woman one of hers.

Triangulation

A writer, her hairdresser, and her therapist all ended up in the same nursing home. Since the writer was on a diet and they were all on a fixed income, the hairdresser and therapist agreed to be paid on a sliding scale of sweet rolls and bowls of tapioca pudding. The writer was still wrestling with her codependency issues. "Don't change because *I* want you to change – change because *you* want you to change," the therapist admonished. "That will be 24 sweet rolls." Flabbergasted at this outrageous overcharge, the writer requested the bill be put on her account, then consulted her journal to find that the therapist had been giving her the same advice for the last 12 consecutive weeks, with a subsequent increase in sweet rolls every time. "Don't worry about it," her hairdresser soothed, while mixing up her blue dye. "Her memory's starting to go – she won't remember how much or whether you've paid her or not." Newly-colored, the writer was more relaxed for her next appointment. "Wow, you've really changed!" the therapist said. "Why, you're almost like a new girl!" The writer smirked, thinking that statement was just more memory loss. But later, looking in the mirror, she saw that her hair was not the usual blue, but an odd mix of purple and pink. "I want my tapioca back!" she demanded of the hairdresser. "But that's been your color for the last 11 years!" the hairdresser protested. Confused, the writer ran back to the therapist.

"Don't let her push you around," the therapist said. "Her boundary issues haven't changed. I saw her for 17 years."

The Perfect Place for Our Pain

Repeatedly doubled-booked out for the rooms they tried to reserve in their community center, a support group had to find new places to meet. One week they met in the children's play area, where the soft toys helped bring up key issues, but a number of the larger members got stuck in the tiny chairs. Another week they met in the furnace room, where the dim lights' meditative effect was unfortunately counteracted by the loud noise of the machinery. Finally they settled on the gym. Although it was also being used by another group, they were able to support themselves creatively by clinging to the ropes that hung from the ceiling.

Accumulation

She'd spent many years letting the chips fall where they may. After a while, they started piling up. Eventually she was living in a house made out of these chips.

Always, Often, Sometimes, Never

She decided to run her life based on statistics. When something terrible happened to her, she fed it into the statistics machine to see how afraid she should be of similar things in the future. Likewise, when something very good occurred, the statistics told her how hopeful she should be of this sort of thing repeating. After a few months, she realized that most of her life was lived at a quotidian. Was this to be her level? She began to stay awake all night, riddled with fear of stagnation.

Boundaries

She'd just been informed she had a rare disease that made it hard to translate almost all of what she said. "I need to go to the colony," she said. "There is no colony," he said, "There's just this rolodex." "Hey, maybe we could start our own!" she said. Quickly, he moved the rolodex away. "I don't give out my clients' names," he said.

Directions

Place your life on a clean, flat surface. Remove outer wrapping. Cut or tear along dotted lines, fold horizontally, and secure edges with tape. Hold at 90-degree angle and apply pressure. Test on an expendable object.

Role Play

Though she loved her cat, she liked telling it, "I don't care about your problems," and she knew full well that the cat didn't care about her problems either. She and the cat were both stand-ins, taking turns being the one with the problems and the one who didn't care. They did this most right after she came back from parties, dates, the DMV, or therapist appointments.

Better by Half

After many years of trying unsuccessfully to lose weight, she finally heard about the strategy of only eating half portions of everything. This strategy was so successful that she started experimenting with other kinds of half measures. She found that she also enjoyed working half-time, believing only half of what people said, and going around half naked. But when she began to do more and more things in a half-assed manner, people started to object, telling her that she'd become half-crazy and should check into a halfway house. Though she took such comments under advisement, she wasn't convinced until someone finally told her that she "might or might not benefit" from such a move. At this point, she found a place, and really enjoyed living there.

LIFE

The Meaning of Life

She spent 12 hours a day sitting at her computer, either working to earn money or working on her resume, till several of her ex-classmates told her to just get a life. She gave up on the resume and got into crocheting, making close to 15 garments in 30 days. Even her best crocheting friends told her to just get a life. She abandoned the crocheting and took up organized religion. The congregation looked at her pityingly. She knew they were thinking she needed to just get a life. That's fine, she thought, and started going out to clubs, drinking or taking drugs almost every night. Eventually even her favorite bartender told her to just get a life. Finally, she divided each day and each week up into various slices, spending a little extra time working to earn money, but dividing the rest of the time about equally between crocheting, religion and going out to clubs. Nobody told her to get a life anymore.

The Party of Your Life

It's hard to tell who might be crashing. People drift in, drift out, show up late, or sometimes disappear. In terms of the refreshments, they're not obviously present; you may need to make some, using spice-rack leftovers and foreign foods in long-expired cans. Same goes for entertainment – you can sing or dance and notice who joins in. If all else fails, there're always projects – no one minds you fixing up the place.

The Journey of My Life

They wanted me to get on the bus, so I did. It was dirty and noisy and dark, with uncomfortable seats. The driver didn't stop when I rang the bell. "Nobody really knows what's out there," he said.

The Watermelon of My Life

It's bright and sweet, but I can't lift it, plus nobody thought to bring a knife.

The Performance of My Life

I'm standing alone on an empty stage with no idea why I'm there, what my role is, or what the audience is expecting me to say. With no better idea, I wing it -- sit down on the edge of the stage and say that I'm open for questions.

BITTERNESS

Kit Bag of Compliments

She'd been living alone in the valley for years, and was overjoyed when General Good Will decided to set up his base there. Not wanting to bother anyone during training time, she waited till a weekend, then went down to the parade ground where the troops went to wander around, smoke cigarettes and hang out. "I'm so glad you're here!" she exclaimed to the first one she met. "This valley has been neglected for years, and I know that your presence will make a wonderful difference!" The soldier looked at her. "Nice hat!" he said, saluted, and walked away. A little disappointed, she waited for the next weekend, which, though rainy, did not deter the more intrepid soldiers from coming out. Again, she timed her walk to intersect with one of them. "How's the battle going?" she asked. "Well, I hope?" The soldier smiled at her and nodded politely. "I like your umbrella," he said, and then went on his way. After this, she stayed in her house for a while, till one day she was startled by the sound of a marching band going right past her door. Flinging it open, she beheld the full army, in all its regalia, standing at a quick parade rest. I'm not going to say anything, she told herself. But she didn't have to, as the General himself turned and gestured at her. "This is a nice smooth roadway you've got here," he said.

The Neverending Boring

Once upon a time, a female prisoner was brought before the king in hopes of being spared. After thinking it over, the king offered to spare her as long as she entertained him with interesting stories. "Can I do a striptease instead?" she asked hopefully. But the king was past that sort of thing. "Nope, stories it is," he proclaimed. "Nobody writes well anymore." She gave a worried frown, but acquiesced, and in due course launched into a ponderous tale about last year's tax returns. "And then what happened?" demanded the king. "I'm afraid that's it," she admitted. He gave her one more chance, only to nearly fall asleep during the gripping saga of a lost and then found cell phone. The king shook his head and looked at her ominously. "I told you this really isn't my skill set," she said. "One more one more," said the king, but the third story was, if anything, even more boring – some recent dream she'd had where someone was chasing her. Sensing her failure, the poor girl was shaking with fear. "You don't deserve to live," the king admonished. "But all the good storytellers are dead or gone. I'll have to make do with you."

Reasonable

Three fairies got together for coffee about once a week as a kind of informal support group. "How's work?" the Green Fairy inquired. "Oh, same as ever," said the Blue Fairy, "trying to get people to make more reasonable wishes. Like last week this woman's wishing she could sell her house. In today's market? What does she expect, a miracle?" "Yeah, last week I got three people wishing they could pay off their student loans," the Silver Fairy said. "Luckily, I got 'em down to half, spaced over a three-year period." "Get this," the Green Fairy said, "the other day I got two people wishing for a job in their field. There was absolutely nothing I could do. I tried to get the social worker to come and work for me, but she wasn't interested." "Well, does anybody have any *good* news?" the Blue Fairy asked? They all sat and thought for a while. "Well, I *was* able to help out this woman who was wishing to be beautiful," the Silver Fairy said. "I granted vacations to the two other women in town who were more beautiful than she was. There's some really great three-week packages to the Ukraine being offered right now."

No Accounting

Jello and Pudding went dancing. They powered through the polka, motored through the merengue, and ended up with the black bottom. Then people started gathering around the dessert table, and they went up arm in arm to get their plates. At the end of the evening, they were still there. "We may be stars on the dance floor, but in terms of taste, we're just not trendy anymore," sighed Pudding. "Don't worry, my sweet," said Jello, taking her in his arms, "at least we'll live to dip another day!" As her head swooped down over the table, a piece of her fell off onto the floor and a stray dog lapped her up. He found her amazingly delicious.

ART

Witnesses

A small town famously noted for its lively arts scene and temperate climate also contained an infamously dangerous intersection of three streets with only two stop signs. An insurance adjuster investigating an accident in the area was delighted to find four witnesses to potentially prove his client's innocence. "I was busking on the corner and heard the whole thing," reported the resident fiddler. "It sounded very much like the final chords of Mark O'Connor's rendition of 'The Devil Went Down to Georgia.'" The adjuster made a note and called the second witness. "I was doing a plein air watercolor and captured the whole thing," reported the resident painter. "The clash of colors after the two vehicles hit almost exactly evoked the colors in De Kooning's study, 'Woman #12.'" The adjuster frowned, made a brief note, and called witness #3. "I was sitting under my poetry tree across the street and transcribed the whole thing," reported the resident poet. "Quote: Your metal meets my tire in a crazed clash of love-fury – our fenders rending as tears flow from both our glove compartments. End quote." The adjuster thanked the poet, but did not make a note this time. Witness #4 didn't answer immediately. "Hello? Is anybody there? I'm calling about the accident." "Hello!" a girl's voice eventually responded. "My housemate saw the whole thing! He's a deaf but talented mime, and I'm a filmmaker. If you want, I'll have him act it out, I'll film him and send you the footage."

Reverse Peep Show

The performance artists enter a building of tiny black box rooms, put their fee in a slot, and activate connection to an on-call audience member. For those performers who are still unable to get off on simply being watched or listened to, responses of varying substantiality are available for additional prorated fees.

How to Bring Forth

"I want to do it naturally," she said. "No pills, no rules, and no formulas." "But what if you get stuck?" she was warned. "Then maybe it just wasn't meant to be." That settled, she set out to find a midwife for her ideas. She was quickly informed that that was called a muse.

Inaccessible-ism

Hoping to experience inspiring art in her town, an artist was profoundly annoyed with an exhibit of a tall stack of miniature tower blocks with writing on the sides that made the topmost blocks impossible to read. In response, she created her own installation of a series of intertwined wall scrawls that started out legible and large but grew increasingly illegible and tiny. The response was immediate: a new installation by a group of provocateurs who hung the entire exhibit of detailed paintings and drawings so close to the top of a tall ceiling that no one could see them as anything more than vague shapes. The next show featured even more detailed paintings and drawings, hung at eye-height but placed in a completely dark room that was illuminated only occasionally by a brief flash of three pinpoint lights. This trend eventually started to die down after the exhibit of fake bus tickets to a town where the installation supposedly was on display.

If I Were in a Catalog

While fine collectibles verge on perfection, fine humans are barely adequate. You ask me how I am. If I am "fine," I'm not in my initial packaging with paperwork intact; rather, my state's some form of undisclosed concern, preoccupation, maybe "slightly foxed."

Performance Art

She wanted to direct a group of site-specific shows – performers in bright-colored suits, odd movements, odder words and music, objects moved in arcane ritual, and optional audience interaction. Alas, nobody ever wants to work for free, so as a cheaper work-around, she started her own cult.

Compilation

She loved making art, but she couldn't commit to a style. After laying out her whole oeuvre end to end, she discovered that she'd recapitulated the entire history of art single-handedly. The best option: a book of "tribute" pieces, dedicated to each of the artists who appeared to have influenced her.

Art Farm

It wasn't the first time, but this was a new day and a new team. Some team members were tasked with straight digging, others turned things over, and still others sweetened the mix. Then arguments started up over choosing the crop. Exotics, natives, or cross-pollination? None of those things had yielded that well in the past. Finally they decided to just go for giant-sized.

Improvisation

"He's acting out again," the babysitter said. "We'll be right over," said the drama teacher. In half an hour, all 16 drama students were queued up at the front door. "He's under the dining room table," the babysitter said. The students joined him there, arranging each other's limbs to make enough room and copying his curled-up posture of head on knees with both arms wrapped around. "Do you need your line?" one of them whispered to him. But there was no response. "Guess it's performance art," another student surmised. Another day, the students came over to join him on the roof, where they found him hurling epithets at passersby. Well-versed in their Shakespeare, they shouted out some good ones, though many of these were lost on the recipients. Finally they arrived to find him throwing items out the window. The babysitter opened some attic junk boxes and handed them various props. "What ho!" they cried, and soon the child's items were lost far down in the pile. At last he ran to his room, and climbed into bed. But the students followed him there. "What shall it be, 'Twelfth Night' or 'Oedipus?'" they asked each other. As he pulled the covers over his head to the strident sounds of the players, he vowed to never ever act out again.

He Might Have Been Framed

"Stop, or I'll draw!" I said, but he didn't stop, so I ran after him with my Number 6 graphite, homing in on his nose, tightening the lines around his head and making his eyes pop out. At last he was finally captured.

Site Specific Installation

Much excitement around the original commission had slowly turned into indifference. The work had been up for so long that it had become virtually invisible to the locals, who forgot to either maintain it or promote it. At his wit's end, the frustrated artist turned it into a site for punk performance art. Several times he set it on fire. Another time he set up some sprinklers and flooded it to the point where only the top part was showing. Other techniques included freezing, tornados, and sending plagues of insects. Of course these radical treatments sped up the existent degrade. Somebody needs to stop him.

The Vision Transfer

"How does inspiration arrive?" he asked the fortune teller. She said it arrived on the bus. "How do I recognize it?" he inquired. "I can't see that far," she told him. Undeterred, he started hanging out at bus stations and bus stops, taking notes and photos. But after several months, he was no further along, and complained mightily to a guy he met at his bar. "Lemme see what you got," the man said, and several dozen photos later, he'd commented approvingly on the cuteness of a handful of subjects. "I work for the transit authority," he said. "These would be perfect for our new promo project. Who knew so many beautiful well-dressed women ride the bus?"

The Rumble

We were kicking some ideas around till finally they lay bleeding in a corner, completely unfit to work. One of them managed to crawl off to get his gang leader, who surprisingly proceeded to kick *us* around till we were in just as bad, if not worse, shape. He then informed us that they all preferred to be pacifists, and that ideas should be approached with an attitude of curiosity and measured inquiry, versus the kind of heedless impetuosity that we were employing. "For example," he said, "What kind of project do you need ideas for?" Alas, by that point, we were too beaten to reply.

Pictionary

A writer and an artist were roommates in an old folks' home. "Hey, I really wish we had one of those things in here," the writer remarked one day. "You know -- it's small and rectangular, you turn it on and music comes out, and you can turn a knob to get different stations." The artist promptly drew an almost photorealistic depiction of the object. "That's it!" cried the writer, "A music box!" Another day, the artist presented the writer with a drawing of some grass. "I really wish they'd let us go out here more often," he complained to the writer. "But what the heck is it called?" "Meadow? Pasture? Field? Land? Foreground?" the writer suggested. "We're getting close," the artist said. "I think it might be foreground."

WORDS

Reading Lessons

Her friend criticized her about the way she read poetry aloud. "Imagine that you're releasing each word firmly but carefully with an eyedropper," suggested her friend. "That way even something like directions on an aspirin bottle can seem freighted with significance."

Ode to Old Pens

My life reflected in this sudden interrupted flow. Why don't I just break down and buy all new? This I won't do, because flow should be free.

Rearrangement

She worked two jobs: one putting words in order, the other putting the containers for the words in order. Alas, she still wasn't able to order her thoughts.

Ghost Writers

A small town determined to maintain its reputation as a literary hot spot poured large amounts of funding into simultaneous writers' residencies. When funding for the project unexpectedly ran out, the townspeople were invited to host the writers themselves. Sadly, not a single townsperson volunteered, so the writers had to find a work-around. Investigating what sounded like squirrels in his attic, a man found a curtain blowing and his grandfather's old typewriter keys unexpectedly dust-free. While spring-cleaning a seldom-used bathroom, a housewife was surprised to find reams of scattered toilet paper with what looked like verses on them. Under the bed: whiskey bottles, cigarettes, a flashlight pen.

Competing with Myself

I caught my clone reading my diary. Another time I caught her being happy on a day when I was crying. The next day she wasn't around. I was just about to call the recall factory when I got a message from her. "Decided to be an independent contractor," it said. "Good luck with everything." Then I started getting weird reports about personal projects I hadn't even applied for yet getting finished by somebody else. That's the last time I leave my diary lying around.

A Fitting End

A fable writer mistakenly submitted his latest piece without including the moral. When he contacted his editor, the editor responded that the piece was perfect as it was, and would be published immediately. When the magazine came out, he got quite a few responses. Fully half his readers loved the piece but interpreted it completely opposite to how it would have been with the moral. Questions for the reader: Does *this* story need a moral? Why or why not? If yes, what should the moral be?

Special Collections

He thought he could read her, but once he'd checked her out, she mostly just sat by his bed. "Where is she?" her old neighbors complained. "Someone either loves her or hates her."

Curiosity Seekers

A writer was excited about going on her first book tour. The first stop was all the way across the country. Because none of the people in that town read themselves, they were happy to be read to. But of course there were no sales. The people in the second town were voracious readers, but only of mysteries. "So who did it?" one of them asked. "Oh -- well, it's open-ended," the writer said. Again, no sales were made. In one of the last towns on the tour, no one appeared to fill up the empty chairs. "How long should we give them?" she asked the organizer. "Oh, lots of them are there already!" the organizer said. "They're just extremely small."

Poems for Schizophrenics

As a poet-on-demand, it's pretty easy to write poems for schizophrenics. You can take virtually any random thing and connect it to virtually any other random thing and they're amazed at how well you read their mind.

Camouflage

Three lines of bad graffiti struck up a friendship on their wall. "How long you been here, bro?" I LOVE CONCHITA inquired of FUCK THE POLICE. "What do you think? Two days!" grumbled FUCK THE POLICE. "And for me, that's pretty long." "Yeah, and when you go, we'll probably go along with you," complained SPECULATOR, "whereas if you weren't here, we might get to see a whole week." "Yeah, yeah, yeah," FUCK THE POLICE growled. "Face it, if we were some sick burners instead of just these lame tags, we might at least get to see the seasons change." After talking all night, they incited each other to move, slowly inching their way around the corner, down onto the pavement, and two blocks over to a gorgeous mural in the alley already defaced by two or three other lines of bad graffiti. "This is where we piggyback!" I LOVE CONCHITA said, as he started to climb up to join them. "Get outta there, you idiot!" SPECULATOR yelled, pulling I LOVE CONCHITA back. "Those guys are vulnerable too! What we do is we go almost up to the top, and then bend around the corners. That way we look like an endorsement."

The Writers' Block Convention

A lecture on how to make excuses, a workshop on how to get your spouse to support you, and, for extra credit, a panel on just how much you can drink before getting thrown out of a bar. Some temporary consternation when one conventioneer came in with not one, but two completely finished novels, but then things were cleared up when the writer stated that both of them had been needing to be re-written for over five years.

A Letter to the Words

Dear Words: I just want to remind you that we don't always have to be on the same page, but we should at least share the theme. And there's no point in arguing about who's better at telling a story and who's better at expressing feelings, because both of us do those things -- at least some of the time. Look – we try to break up, and it never works for that long. Part of the problem might be that we don't have the same love language. You're out there lining things up, while I tend to go round and round. But it all comes from the same place! Remember when we first met? How instantly joined we felt, and how everyone loved us together? I hope you're well, but I hope you're thinking of me – I know I'm thinking of you. Especially at night, when I look up at the moon and start crying, wondering what you'd say. Sincerely yours, The Music.

Recombinations

We were desperate for new sentences. Both our outside sentence man and our inside sentence woman were old and close to their term, and thus often distracted. Piles of unswept-up words lay on the lawn, and participles dangled casually over the neighbors' fence. Inside, unnoticed words gathered dust in corners and beneath the furniture, and clumps of random words lingered on the stairs where our tongues often tripped over them. Finally we broke down and called our old agency, only to discover an unhelpful new glut of sentence gig workers: everyone doing it, no one doing it well. After some hesitation, we determined to start trying to do it ourselves. How had we managed all those years ago, before we'd relied on our help? Not sure which words were keepers, we didn't know what to throw out, yet it took us all day to simply put one phrase together.

ANNOUNCEMENTS

Email Response from the "I Don't Know Club" President

We were sorry to hear of your cancellation request. Please know that we value your name in our roster of ABD students, baton droppers, failed quiz contestants and devil's advocates. Our records report that you dropped membership and were subsequently put back no less than 70 times. You should know that few members are as overpaid in their dues, in our "he who hesitates is lost" value system. This makes your membership good for the next 30 years.

Invitation to the Festival of Negativity

Mark your calendars now for this year's Negativity Fest! As promised, we'll have our usual negativity queen, negativity bouncy house, and negative face painting. Stroll the grounds to the sounds of our negativity minstrels, bowing their cellos with minor, discordant strains. Be amazed at the feats of Negator the Magnificent, as he juggles 5 jobs, 2 ex-wives, 7 children, and a budding career as a rock star. Such complex and creative forms are seldom seen outside of such a fest. In fact, it's not unusual for our guests to get overwhelmed, so as usual we'll have our decompression booth outside the grounds, where you can ramp the atmosphere gradually up to neutral.

Email to the Members of the Word Association

Hope all of you are ready for our annual meeting! We have more prospective new words than ever this year, so have your ballots ready! As we hope you remember from last year, all new words must not only be sponsored in by existing words, but have plausible affiliation. For example, the words "cat" and "bag" are affiliated, but the words "mother" and "tirade" are not, despite what your psychiatrist may have said. Another reminder for those of you who are new: Please do not nominate "and" and "the," no matter how well you know them. There are plenty of other places those words can go. We reserve the right to prioritize uncommon words.

Advertisement for the Self-Publishers' Clearing House

Come on -- admit it! The layout looks cheap, the font size is wrong, and the type lines are too small to read. You know you have dozens of copies stacked up in those boxes downstairs, and you've already given the others away for free. Sure, you might make new friends someday who might want a copy or two, or you might get famous somehow and the signed ones might go through the roof. But who are you kidding? Admit you need help! Let us come to your house and take all those copies away.

Bad Haircut Condolence Card

Sometimes we don't put together the fact that we're too close to the edge until that definitive moment when it's too late. Who knows why these things happen? Maybe someone was hungover or exhausted from an all-nighter. Supposedly God keeps track of every hair, but even He has His off days. Your loss is regrettable, unfortunate and unfair. Enclosed please find a coupon for a *good* salon – I don't advise going back to that cut-rate place.

Advertisement for the Self-Publishers' Clearing House

Come on -- admit it! The layout looks cheap, the font size is wrong, and the type lines are too small to read. You know you have dozens of copies stacked up in those boxes downstairs, and you've already given the others away for free. Sure, you might make new friends someday who might want a copy or two, or you might get famous somehow and the signed ones might go through the roof. But who are you kidding? Admit you need help! Let us come to your house and take all those copies away.

The Termagant Machine

Tired of aggressive and overly critical neighbors, family members and co-workers? The Termagant Machine could be the answer to your prayers! Contained in a handy pocket-sized box, the machine activates with the press of a button to unleash a life-sized, realistic-looking 3D termagant who will instantly launch into a variety of rants, excoriations and harangues. Comes with a default set and is also programmable. (Please be advised that should your target retaliate by launching his or her own termagant, resulting shorts could damage both products. Termagantmachine.com cannot be held responsible for the ensuing results.)

JOKES

Useful

I would order it if it were orderable: an epipen for angst.

Best Western

A depressive, a man with Parkinson's and an accident-prone man all walked into the bar of a hotel that was hosting an NRA convention. Nevertheless, all their guns were confiscated.

Invisible Siamese Twin

Just when I'm caught up in the moment, she points out the larger picture. "Who *are* all these people?" she says.

Insubstantial

After a big dinner, I like to enjoy an apercu or two. But you can't make a meal out of them.

Three Very Short Stories About Vampires

I

A vampire found an old copy of "How to Win Friends and Influence People" in a used bookstore. "Seems a little dated, but there still might be some relevant stuff in here," he said to himself.

II

A vampire bought a new house and found out within a couple months that it was riddled with termites. "I thought they did an inspection!" he fumed. "My basement wood boxes are ruined!"

III

A vampire was having trouble with his phone and brought it into the phone store. "It looks like you're out of minutes," the phone salesman said. "That's never happened to me before in my life!" the vampire said.

Pillow on the Kitchen Counter

Given that the sleep of reason produces monsters, she determined to start sleeping unreasonably.

Three Very Short Meaningful Stories

I

You run into three different meanings at a cocktail party, each wearing a completely different outfit. Are they all here for the same party, or did they stumble in here by mistake? Either way, they all seem to be enjoying themselves.

II

You usually get my meanings, and I usually get yours. But sometimes some of your meanings are a little too long in the sleeves. And you always complain that my bright red meaning clashes with your orange and black hat.

III

Two meanings from the same neighborhood checked themselves into the rehab center and came out utterly changed. In fact, they were like new. Almost no one recognized them, but for the moles on their feet. Later, it was discovered that both of the meanings had been born to the same mother.

DEBATABLE

Who Really Knows

Intention and Motivation were sitting around discussing whether the end justifies the means. "Hey, we should ask Reward and Punishment," said Intention. "They're sitting right over there." "Good idea," said Motivation. "Hey, Punishment," he called, "How's it hangin'?" "I'm actually Reward," one of them said. "We switch our clothes all the time." "OK, whatever," Motivation said. "Listen, where do you guys stand on the whole ends and means deal?" "Well, it all depends on the long term," Punishment said. "Sometimes you get rewarded right away and then get punished later. Or it could go vice versa. You know, the very question means somebody smells a rat." "You might wanna talk this over with Cause and Effect," remarked Reward. "They just walked in the door." "Why not?" Intention said, and waved to get their attention. Effect raised his glass in a toast, but by the time they'd made their way over, Cause had vanished. "He's kinda hard to pin down," Effect apologized. Intention bought a drink for both of them just in case. "Tonight we're trying to nail down this ends and means thing," he reported. "Seems like you guys might have some thoughts on this." "Ah, yes," said Effect. "But you see, it's complicated. Say you've got a great scheme, but it has some collateral damage. Now, that might seem like a direct cause and effect, but what caused you to come up with the scheme in the first place? Are you justified if you're just acting on beliefs that got passed down to you in good faith?" Intention and Motivation were getting frustrated. "Sorry – that's all I got," Effect admitted. "But let me introduce you to the new girl behind the bar. Her name is Interpretation. She wears her hair a million different ways."

Fair Play and Turnabout

Thesis and Antithesis were hanging out at the rec center drinking Cokes and shooting some pool. "Blah, blah, blah, appropriation, blah, blah, corporatization, blah, blah, blah, the patriarchy," expounded Thesis, the way she'd done hundreds of times. "You could be right," observed Antithesis slowly. Thesis laid down her cue and gaped at him. "That's not what you *usually* say!" she said in astonishment. Antithesis sighed. "Why so much polarization?" he lamented. "It's tiresome and extreme." "But we *need* polarization!" she protested. "Otherwise we're too wishy-washy!" At that point, Antithesis ceremoniously removed his "A"-emblazoned ball cap and presented it to her. Then he racked the balls and shot them in all directions.

THE WORLD

Postcard from the Home Planet

So sorry you didn't make it. We barely made it ourselves. One of us lost his foot as the door was closing. It's really beautiful here -- a lot like it was down there before they wrecked it. We've petitioned the rescuers to come and get you, but the list is really long, and as more of us get born, it gets even longer. Wish you were here.

Weather Wars

Wind, Clouds and Sun are suing for plagiarism. The game of "Rock, Paper, Scissors" is suspiciously close to the game these entities have played for thousands of years. Clouds cover sun, wind blows away clouds, and sun takes wind chill away.

The Hokey Pokey

Test the waters, come back and engage. Of what does this shaking consist? Make love, make war, work, play, or celebrate. You come into this place and look around, see who is there. How will you dance yourself this time around?

The Diary of the Sun

May 29th: Came out for a while, but got bored. Spent the rest of the day in bed. June 15th: Heard about an important event. Should I make an appearance? Not sure. June 18th: Blew off the picnic day, which was probably a mistake. Because they cancelled it, the guy didn't get to propose, so the girl took the overseas contract after all. There's so much pressure on me! August 17th: Dog days! Your unoiled shins will bark with alizarin graze! September 8th: Showed up for my first therapy appointment. My therapist has to wear dark glasses, so I can't tell what she really thinks of me. Chart says I have a guilt complex and also anger issues. December 19th: I felt like putting on a show today. Ice crystals glittering in my shine, snow-dazzled people blinking and shielding their eyes from my light. March 21st: Came in and went out a couple hundred times. My therapist thinks I probably have ADD.

Universal Complaint

I get really tired of people blaming things on me. How'd you like it if I said, "I felt like Sue was telling me to quit my job," or "I felt like Joe was telling me to go to Bali?" Just because I'm big, complex and mysterious doesn't mean I automatically go around telling people to do things. And I take responsibility for my decisions! But from now on I'm going to maintain a blame game too. I felt like the cosmos was telling me to give you this notification.

Party Now It's 2099

They finally asked us to leave, complaining that we ate too much of the food, prowled the basement and attic rooms searching for hidden gems, and tossed our trash on the lawn. Clearly we need to find a less uptight planet.

GOD

Our Father's Lament

It's really hard to be a single parent. They're out there playing in the dark, hungry, dirty and exhausted, and still refuse to come in. I've called them till my throat has gotten hoarse. You know how they get – so wound up that they just can't stop. They've got their toys, plus that stuff they built down there -- I don't even know what it is. Look at that one, with the long white beard, dragging his oxygen tank – what are you gonna do? I fixed the place up really nice for them. You think they care?

Side Effects

They were wandering lost in the dark, sick and confused. So you built them a number of different lit-up theme rooms so that they'd have a choice. Not surprisingly, most of them chose the more easily habitable rooms. But in the giddiness of these expansions, the overpopulation ramped up fast. At that point, they started having less enjoyable kinds of choices -- say, between a claustrophobic New York subway theme room or a more breathable but freezing Arctic tundra theme room. To try to at least get something more out of the second category, they started to use those rooms for industry instead of habitation. But then the lights in the industry rooms slowly began to go out, and eventually the entire electrical system began to be affected. You watched helplessly as more and more people began again to wander in the dark, sick and confused.

Unearthed

One of the new gods was landscaping his yard when his spade hit a metal box. Because its label was in a strange language, he took it to a language expert before he opened it. Several weeks later, he got the label back with its translation: "Time Capsule: The Earth and a couple hundred stars."

Our Scriptwriter's Lament

I just couldn't make these characters work the way I wanted them to. Right now I keep all my rough drafts inside this bottom drawer. Once in a while I hear some noise down there. They're frustrated, half-finished, want some kind of resolution, but I'm tired. They will have to wait a few more centuries.

UNEASY

The Black Hole Cafe

Beware of taking your guests to the Black Hole Café. This place tends to disappear people, either immediately or not too far down the road. The tricky thing about the Black Hole Café is it's not even called the Black Hole Café – that would be bad for business. The other tricky thing is that it's in different locations. Maybe you yourself actually work for the Black Hole Café as a kind of double agent. Look for it at a location very near you.

Companion Animal

In the bus with you, its eyes bulge as it squats in its cage. Strapped to your bike, it slides back and forth on the turns. Let loose in the house, it runs from you, but you catch it and hold it and put it in place on your lap. Nibbling its lettuce, it knows you and will stay with you -- as long as you don't let it out.

Distribution Center

One day when I was wandering the corridors, I stumbled on the office of the Baby Coalition. File drawers were everywhere. At first it was confusing. Then I started to figure it out. Just like any other government office, everyone gets a file at birth, but in this case it was just the females, and the files were sorted in a certain way. The label on one file drawer read: "PEOPLE WHO REALLY NEED A DISTRACTING, COMPELLING PROJECT." Another read: "YOU CAN'T ALWAYS GET WHAT YOU WANT." A third read: "DODGED THE BULLET." Of course I seized the opportunity to look up my mother's file. It read: "BE CAREFUL WHAT YOU WISH FOR."

The Unexpected

Always, Often, Sometimes and Never went on a beach vacation to the Oregon coast. Always and Never were codependent twins who sometimes switched identities, while Sometimes and Often were relativists who occasionally switched roles. Sometimes attempted to drag Never into the waves, while Often and Always walked peacefully arm in arm. They'd just settled down in their favorite picnic spot when a woman approached the group, introducing herself as Once. Looking furtively at each other, they quickly began to pack up their things. All of them feared what she might do.

FATE

Fixer-Upper

I died and went straight to hell. But it wasn't nearly as hellish as I'd expected -- chipped grottoes like worn-out spooky fun-fair rides, eternal flames that perpetually died, and pitchforks so blunted from use that they barely even broke the skin anymore. "It was great 100 years ago, but then we ran out of funds," a minor demon admitted. "Any suggestions? We always ask the new blood." As a starving artist, I knew a few things about how to work on a shoestring. In a couple of months, I'd turned the place around.

Limbo

In a rush to try to visit her friend, she was put on a standby flight list. With extra time to kill, she decided to see a musical matinee. Because it was the weekend, there were lines, so she got on the waiting list. Not having had time for lunch, she waited in line for a hot pretzel, only to see the last one vanish just as her number came up. "Let me make it up to you," the pretzel vendor said. "My cousin will do your nails for free. She's right across the street." There was a bit of a line at the nail salon, but the chairs were so comfortable that she promptly fell asleep. When she woke up, she was back in the standby line.

Purgatory

I'm standing alone on an empty stage with no idea why I'm there, what my role is, or what the audience is expecting me to say. With no better idea, I wing it -- sit down on the edge of the stage and say that I'm open for questions.

Spoiled for Choice

The next place was both more and less than I thought it would be. The first thing I got was a menu with housing options. But none of the houses had roofs, and when I inquired if I could have one in exchange for a floor, I was informed that there were no substitutions. Next, I was directed to another menu, but none of the men came with hearts. I asked if I could swap out for an arm or a leg, but no, there were no substitutions. Having waited too long to decide, I myself became a menu option, but as you might expect, all of us women were lacking. One of the men who perused us wondered if he could trade out our good posture for a couple of larger breasts, but before he could get the predictable reply, I took great pleasure in informing him that there were no substitutions.

ENDINGS

Marathon

This morning's thoughts burst into the day like fresh horses finding a place amongst the ones already running. Some of the older ones have died, but their bones are still in the field.

Turnover

She went in and was disappointed to see that the place had already changed hands. The new owner guessed this from her expression and smiled at her anyway. "One minute," he said, going into the storeroom. He came back out holding out a box. "Your memories!" he exclaimed. "We saved them for you!" Somewhat comforted by the gesture, she thanked him and went home. But no sooner had she finally started adjusting to the new place, than it changed hands once again. Her only choice was to request a new box. Conveniently, the new box also contained her memories of the previous place. Though it was a challenge to layer one associated memory of a place with another associated memory of a different version of the same place, she did her best. This kept happening. The boxes kept getting bigger, filling up the storeroom and spilling out into the main room. On her last visit, the box was so big that it filled the entire space.

The Vanishing

I passed two chocolate cakes by the side of the road. The next day there was only one. "I really miss her," the cake was heard to lament. "It's just not a celebration anymore."

Diminishing Returns

When he was small, everyone always told him to always watch out for strangers. When he asked what a stranger was, he was told, "someone we haven't introduced you to." As he grew older, his group began to die off, till only a handful were left. Finally, only a decrepit elder remained, who was so feeble that she could barely speak. At last she was on her death bed. Before she died, he tried to make out her words. It was something about strangers. It was something about kindness.

About the Author:

Melanie Reed is a writer and visual artist with a creative writing BA from the University of Washington. Publication credits include speculative fiction/psychological suspense novella "Every Other Day" (Hiraeth Books, 2021), and 2018 graphic novel/epic poem/soul collage book artwork "The Scrapbook of Dreams" (University of Washington's Suzzallo Library special collections). She lives in Seattle, Washington.

EVERY OTHER DAY

In this novel, Graham Greenaway, a 48-year-old financial consultant from Chicago, suddenly finds that he's transported into an alternate world every other day. Stunned and confused, he tries to ground himself by keeping a diary of his experiences in these worlds, each of which challenges him in a different way.

To order a copy of her novella "Every Other Day," go here:

> https://www.hiraethsffh.com/product-page/every-other-day-by-melanie-reed

www.ingramcontent.com/pod-product-compliance
Lightning Source LLC
LaVergne TN
LVHW012023060526
838201LV00061B/4423